ADVENTURE DUCK

VS

THE ARMADILLO ARMY

BY STEVE COLE

ILLUSTRATED BY ALEKSEI BITSKOFF

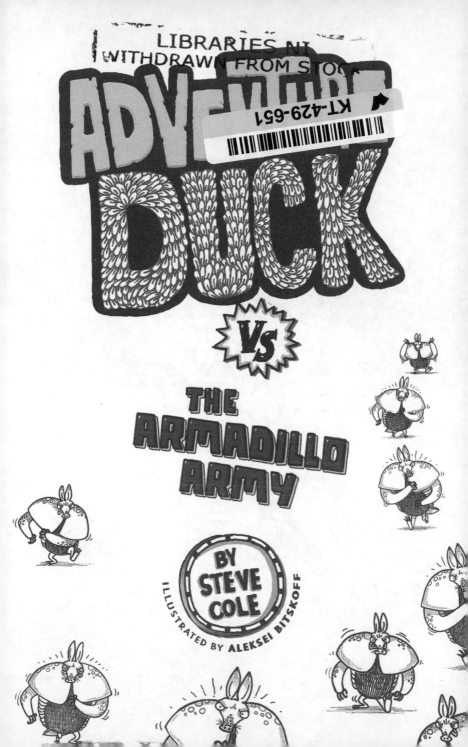

1

Superheroes
in Training

One night, in a park not far from here, a
duck in a superhero costume stood face
to face with a glowing, pink-striped zebra.
Raising his wings, the duck flew at the
zebra in a *KUNG-FU ATTACK*.
The zebra rolled aside and fired **sizzling**
blasts from her front hooves, missing the
duck's tail feathers by millimetres.

"Hey, Ziggy!" quacked the duck. "I thought
we agreed not to attack each other's butts?"

"What's the matter – scared of getting yours kicked?" Ziggy said, grinning. "It's important to be prepared. As the newest superheroes in town we have to practise our powers ..." She flexed her muscles and her pink stripes turned electric orange. "AND NEON ZEBRA IS READY FOR ACTION."

"So is Adventure Duck," the duck added.

"QUACK!"

With a supersonic quack that made the entire park tremble, he kicked a nearby litter bin with one webbed foot.

WHUMP! The bin rocketed up into the sky! Luckily, Adventure Duck – or A.D. for short – was super-fast as well as super-strong. He whizzed right up into the air, overtook the speeding litter bin, turned it round and rode it back down to earth.

"Yay!" Ziggy grinned. "Target practice!" Aiming at A.D. she fired more electric zaps from her hooves.

"So that's how it is, huh?" Adventure Duck dived inside the bin as pink explosions boomed all around him. "Well, two can play at that game!" Still inside the litter bin, he shot across the park – aiming straight at Ziggy.

"HIIIIIII-YAH!" Stripes blazing bright red now, Neon Zebra jumped into the air, karate-kicked the bin and cracked it open in a shower of sparks.

A.D. burst out in a shower of trash and launched his ultimate attack – a tickle fight! "Who's laughing now?" he said, shaking his super-tickly wing feathers right in Ziggy's face.

- - - - - -

Neon Zebra was soon wailing and snorting with helpless laughter. "Stop!" she shouted, wriggling and giggling. Then she pointed her hoof behind him. "Hey, is that soggy bread in the water?"

"WHERE?" cried A.D., turning round to look. Soggy bread was his favourite snack!

ZAAAAP! Neon Zebra zapped the distracted duck right in the butt with her hoof.

"**YEOOWWWW!**" A.D. went somersaulting through the air and landed with a sizzling splash in the middle of the pond.

- - - - -

"Direct hit!" Neon Zebra chortled.

"Direct hot, you mean." A.D. said, shaking his soggy, scorched tail feathers off to dry them.

"*UGH!*" Ziggy spluttered as the drips of water sent sparks shooting from her neon stripes.

"Training is over," said a deep, mystical voice that bubbled up from beneath A.D. "You must now use your skills to defeat ... **EVIL!**"

The next thing A.D. knew, he was rising slowly into the air – pushed up by a large, levitating egg. The egg was speckled green, with eyes that were wise and a massive white moustache that was possibly even wiser.

"Hey, Yoki," said Ziggy. "What's up?"

"I am!" A.D. complained, flapping his wings. **"Put me down, egg-head."**

"Down – and up – are but illusions, young duck," said Yoki calmly.

- - - - -

A.D. sighed. Just weeks ago, his life had been oh-so-ordinary. But when a weird meteorite landed in the duck pond, things quickly turned **QUACKERS**!

The rock had been full of space energy that turned Yoki from a regular egg into a mega-moustachioed mutant – and turned A.D. from an ordinary duck into a **superhero**. Other chunks of the meteor had fallen all over the world – including the one that splash-landed in Ziggy's watering hole and turned her into a **NEON ZEBRA**!

"You know, Yoki," said A.D., "you might be a wise guru, a super-smart scientist—"

"And a mystical master as one with the universe," Yoki suggested.

"Yeah, but I'll tell you this – you make a lousy cushion!" A.D. hopped off Yoki, rubbed his sore bottom and paddled back to Ziggy. "Now, what's all this about having to defeat evil?"

"**Danger is afoot**," Yoki warned the superheroes in a booming voice. "**I can feel it in my moustache**."

"You can feel a *foot* in your moustache?" Ziggy frowned.

- - - - -

"I'm talking about a danger to the whole world." Yoki floated over to some nearby reeds. "Come with me to the **UNDERPOND** and I will explain!"

Adventure Duck and Ziggy hurried to follow Yoki. One of the reeds was a lever in disguise, and as Yoki yanked it with his moustache, the ground tipped upside down. A.D. and Ziggy dropped into a large underground chamber. Controls and switches stuck out from the feathery floor and strange gadgets hung down from the muddy roof. There was also a games console, a gym and an enormous TV, so the off-duty superheroes could relax in comfort.

- - - - -

A.D. hurried to the soggy-bread dispenser built into one wall. "Stick on the cartoon channel, Zig!" he cried. "After all that training I'm ready to veg out in front of the telly. Or bread out, anyway!"

"We will watch the World News," Yoki declared.

"World *snooze*, more like!" moaned A.D.

Ziggy tapped the TV with an electric hoof and it sparked into life. Pictures of a rainforest with its trees knocked down like skittles appeared on the screen. "What happened there?" she wondered.
"A hurricane?"

- - - - - -

"Experts cannot explain what caused such widespread damage to this rainforest ..." came the news reporter's voice.

"**Boring!**" A.D. broke in through a beakful of bread. He flicked the channel to a superhero cartoon, but Ziggy switched it back.

"Yoki's right," Ziggy said. "We need to know what's going on in the world."

"In other news, sweet shops were wrecked last night in cities across Mexico," the reporter went on. *"Police suspect the destruction may be the work of vigilante dentists ..."*

- - - - -

"Chocolate's not good for animals, so who cares?" A.D. yawned and settled down for a nap. "Wake me up when there's a shortage of breadcrumbs."

"DANGER!" yelled Yoki. His mystical moustache twitched and bounced like twenty tiny kittens chasing balls of wool. "I sense another **METEOR MUTANT** at work."

"Another superhero like us?" asked Ziggy.

- - - - -

Yoki shook his head. "The same meteorites have given it powers," he said gravely. "But it has chosen to use its abilities for evil. You must go to Mexico at once, young heroes – **AND STOP IT!**"

Mission to Mexico

"I can't fly to Mexico now, omelette-face!" A.D. complained. "I've been training half the night. I'm too tired to go thousands of miles with an annoying electric zebra on my back."

"**ANNOYING?**" Ziggy growled, putting on her lightning bolt bandana. "Say that again and I'll turn you into **crispy duck!**"

"I know you are both tired," said Yoki, hovering between them. "But fear not!" He picked up two pairs of glasses with his moustache. "With these you can travel at supersonic speed even in your sleep."

"It's the middle of the night," said Ziggy, slipping on the shades. "Why would we need to wear sunglasses—? **WHOA!**" Sleek steel jets slid out from behind the frames, pointing past her ears.

"**WOW!**" A.D. grabbed the other pair. "**SHADES WITH BUILT-IN ROCKET BOOSTERS?**"

"And 100 per cent UV protection," said Yoki proudly. "I call them **Jet-Shades**. Steered by the power of my mind, they will take you anywhere!"

Minutes later, looking cool in their Jet-Shades, Adventure Duck and Neon Zebra were shooting through the night.

"**WHEEEEEEEEEEEEEEE!**" Ziggy shouted.

"Don't you *DARE* wee, I'm flying right behind you!" A.D. yelled back. Then he spoke to Yoki with his mind, using the

- - - - - -

Egg-stra Sensory Perception link they shared. "Oi, egg-head. When we reach Mexico, what are we looking for?"

"Search for an animal acting oddly," said Yoki.

A.D. watched Ziggy twirl through the air like a stripy spinning top. "I think I've found one already."

He swooped down to avoid getting lashed by Ziggy's tail – and almost crashed into a massive billboard! As he whizzed past he grimaced at the sight of the tiny flat-faced dog dressed in carnival gear grinning out from it.

- - - - -

"*POWER PUG*," A.D. muttered.

The cute little pug was the famous face
of a huge global food and drink empire:
Poocho, Inc. But when the meteorites had
fallen, he'd gained powers of mind control.
Power Pug had put himself in charge of
the company and tried to take over the
world with mind-control milkshakes. A.D.
and Ziggy had dealt with the demented
dog in the end – but who knew what other
crazed super-creatures were out there?

With the Jet-Shades propelling them
along, the journey to Mexico sped by.
A.D. managed to catch forty winks, but was
woken by another near miss – this time,

with a jumbo jet. That put him off sleeping
... even though Ziggy's tuneless singing put
him off staying awake!

Oh! Off to Mexico-co-co

We go-go-go-go-go-go-go

To find an evil foe-foe-foe

And break his toe-toe-toe-toe-toe

And then his elbow-bow-bow-bow

And belly butto-to-to-to ... n

"That's the worst song I ever heard!" A.D.
groaned. "How can anyone break a belly
button?"

- - - - -

"With practice," Ziggy suggested.

The day grew hotter and a pretty Mexican town came into sight – a jumble of colourful houses, ornate old buildings, parks and piazzas. The smell of tacos and tortilla chips wafting up from the town made Adventure Duck's beak water.

Yoki's voice boomed in his head. "I sense the mutant's presence!"

Below them, men and women were charging out of a large candy shop named **CHOCO MERCADO**, screaming in terror. The store's walls were shaking and the roof was rattling.

- - - - -

"Hey!" Ziggy shouted. "I can hear people screaming."

"Maybe the mutant's just got a sweet tooth," said A.D, gulping. "Neon Zebra, are you ready for action?"

"**STRIPED AND HYPED!**" Ziggy's stripes fired up, bright orange. "How about you, Adventure Duck?"

"**Ready, steady, soggy bready!**" A.D. adjusted his red underpants. "**Let's go!**"

As the last of the panicking people ran outside, A.D. and Ziggy landed and switched

- - - - -

off their Jet-Shades. They burst into the store and A.D. could see that almost every aisle had been attacked. The shelves were stripped bare of chocolate. Gummy sweets, dolly mixture and jelly beans were scattered all over the floor. Even the café at the back had been smashed up. Huge, simmering vats of chocolate and caramel sauce for ice-cream sundaes had spilled out on to the floor in sticky puddles.

"Our new meteor mutant really made a mess in here," said Ziggy.

"It's a shame he didn't damage those." A.D. pointed to some colourful piñatas shaped like Power Pug. "Hmm, perhaps I'll save him the effort." **BAM!** He karate-chopped a piñata with one wing and the candy-containing canine cracked open, spilling chocolates everywhere. "That's better," A.D. declared. "I think I'll trash another."

"NO, YOU WON'T!" came a deep, throaty bellow from across the factory. *"I DECIDE WHAT GETS DESTROYED AROUND HERE."*

Adventure Duck and Neon Zebra stared as a scaly ball the size of a tank rolled into sight – and uncurled into an incredible beast. First a pointed, bumpy head poked

- - - - -

out, crowned with a red beret. Then came four enormous feet with terrifying claws. Matted hair hung down from its belly to brush the floor, and a powerful tail flicked about behind it. The creature glared at them like some terrifying prehistoric monster.

"What is it?" A.D. whispered.

"Ugly," Ziggy said.

"It's a giant armadillo!"

Yoki's voice boomed through A.D.'s head. "Beware – his strength, claws and super-tough shell make him a deadly opponent."

"Get out of here, fools," the creature grunted,

- - - - - -

"or face the wrath of *ARMANDO ...*
THE COMMANDO!"

"Armando the Commando?" A.D. echoed.
"Seriously?"

"Nice beret, dude!" Ziggy said, laughing.
"You look like something that fell out of
GODZILLA'S BUTT and joined the
army!"

Armando's bright green eyes narrowed.
"Get out of my way."

"Look, *hombre*." Adventure Duck bravely
stepped towards the giant armadillo. "We
know you've been transformed by a lump

- - - - -

of space rock, because it happened to us too. But you don't have to be a bad guy, Armando. Why are you trashing chocolate shops?"

"Because I got bored of smashing down rainforests," Armando grunted.

Ziggy and A.D. exchanged looks.

"We heard about that on the news," Ziggy said. "So you're responsible for all that damage too?"

"Exactly." Armando nodded proudly. "And now I'm going to damage *you*!" Eyes glowing brighter, he rolled up into

- - - - -

a giant scaly ball and hurled himself towards them. *"PREPARE TO BE FLATTENED!"*

Mexican Mayhem

A.D. quacked with horror as the giant armoured animal came thundering towards him. He dodged aside and bashed into Ziggy, knocking her clear. Armando hurtled past and crashed into a shelf of chocolate biscuits, crushing them into crumbs.

"That was close," Ziggy panted.

"That was **FUN**." Armando laughed
and shot forward again, propelled by his
powerful tail.

"*EAT MY SPARKS!*" Neon Zebra
fired bright orange crackles of energy
from her fluorescent hooves. Armando lit
up like a glow-in-the-dark bowling ball
but kept on rolling, unharmed.

"My turn!" A.D. flew over and struck the armadillo with his webbed feet. "OWWW!" He bounced off helplessly and crashed into the checkouts. He'd used all his strength, but barely even slowed Armando down!

"That does it, you barmy-dillo. I'm going nuclear on your butt!" Ziggy charged up her stripes to ruby red and yelled her battle cry: "**NEON ZEBRA-RA-RA-RA-RA-RA-RAAAAAAH!**" A brilliant blast of energy blazed from her front hooves ...

But the armadillo could not be stopped! He bashed into Ziggy and sent her flying into the store café. She crashed hooves-first into a table and fell to the floor, landing in a

- - - - - -

puddle of gloopy caramel sauce.

"**ZIGGY!**" A.D. felt anger flush though his feathers. "Are you OK?"

"Try worrying about yourself!" Like a giant wrecking ball, Armando rolled towards Adventure Duck, turning the shelves in his path to sawdust. Desperately, A.D. tried tickle-tactics. He jumped over Armando and wiggled his tail feathers over the animal's hide. But the giant beast didn't so much as giggle.

"It's no good," Ziggy groaned, her stripes smothered in sticky caramel. "He's too thick-skinned."

- - - - -

"Hey, Armando! Why are you wearing that beret on your bum?" A.D. shouted. "Whoops, my mistake – it's your head!"

Armando just shrugged off the insult.

"You're right, Zig," Adventure Duck said, sighing. "He really *IS* thick-skinned!"

The sound of wailing sirens came from outside. Ziggy smiled. "Somebody's called the cops!"

"I don't answer to the police," Armando announced. "I am a commando. **I only take orders from my general.**"

"Who's that?" A.D. frowned.

But Armando wasn't listening. He bounced
high into the air, stuck out his claws –
and drilled right through the floor. Mud,
rock and dirt came flying out from the
hole as he dug a tunnel at super-speed
and vanished from sight. The whole store
rocked, and a Power Pug piñata fell down
and landed on A.D.'s head.

"Huh? It's **YOU!**" he heard Ziggy cry
dizzily. "**I'LL GET YOU, PUG
BRAIN!**"

"**No, Zig! Don't fire.
It's me!**" A.D. pulled frantically

- - - - -

at the piñata but – *ZAP!* Neon energy

blasted him across the store.

He struck the wall and

the piñata broke

open. "Well, that's

one way of

getting the

stupid

thing off!"

"A.D.?" Ziggy

blinked, sitting in a

caramel puddle. "Sorry, I thought you were

Power Pug – that armadillo arma-dazed

me!"

"I'm afraid he's got away." Adventure

Duck flapped over to inspect the hole, choking on dust and dirt. "Yep. He's gone underground!"

Ziggy's stripes blazed angry neon pink, burning off the caramel sauce – and singeing A.D.'s cape. "No one makes a crème brûlée out of me and gets away with it!" she said. "Let's go!" Ziggy leapt through the hole and Adventure Duck dived after her.

BUMP*!* He landed on top of Ziggy. "Sorry," A.D. said, blinking blindly. "It's so dark down here I can't see a thing."

"I'll see what I can do," said Ziggy.

- - - - -

FLASH! She lit up the darkness with her luminous yellow stripes.

A.D. and Ziggy waddled and trotted through the freshly dug tunnel.

It stretched on for ages, winding and twisting deep underground. But there was no sign of Armando.

"That overgrown **gobstopper** has vanished," A.D. said, sighing. "He said he only took orders from his general. I wonder who that is?"

"I have no clue," said Ziggy. "My general knowledge is **AWFUL!**"

- - - - -

Adventure Duck and Ziggy pressed on, until screams and wails drifted down from somewhere above them. "Sounds like more trouble. Maybe he's destroying another candy store?" said A.D.

"Messing with all that candy, he'll need a filling – and I'm happy to oblige!" Ziggy blasted a hole in the rocky ceiling above them with an electric zap. Adventure Duck whisked her away through the hole, ready for battle.

But there was no sign of danger above ground. The wailing they'd heard was actually a mariachi band playing in a busy town square. The screams came

- - - - - -

from excited children whacking sweets from another Power Pug-shaped piñata, this one hanging from a tree. The whole place was in full fiesta mode! No one seemed terribly surprised to find a zebra and a duck wandering about; it simply added to the carnival feel. People were dancing to the band's music, or buying delicious food from the bustling stalls.

"Zig," said Adventure Duck, "do you think it's bad for a superhero's image to peck around on the ground for tasty scraps?"

"Yes," Ziggy replied.

"Then look the other way!" A.D. started

- - - - -

gobbling up fallen tortilla chips from
the ground. "*Om, nom, nom ...*
ARGH*!*" He flapped
up in the air, eyes
bulging, gasping for air.
"Chilli on those chips!
Mouth burning! MY
TONGUE IS ON FIRE—!"

SPLASH! Something sticky drenched
A.D. in mid-air. "Ugh! What just happened?"

Ziggy stared across the square at a strange,
stocky animal; it looked like a camel who'd
lost its hump and fallen in a barrel of fluff.
"That llama just spat at you – from all the
way over there!"

- - - - - -

The llama, who was carrying a bundle of blankets, quickly ran over. "Are you OK?" she asked brightly. "I heard you say you were on fire so I spat on you to put it out."

"I didn't mean it literally!" Adventure Duck shook his feathers crossly. "My mouth was burning after a hot tortilla chip."

"Oh. Sorry." The llama looked sad. "I was only trying to help. I'm Lola, by the way."

"I'm Ziggy," said Ziggy.

"I'm soaked," said A.D.

"How did you even hear Adventure Duck,
Lola?" Ziggy wondered. "You were on the
other side of the square."

"Well!" Lola lowered her voice. "You
probably won't believe me, but this rock
fell from outer space and it ... like ...

CHANGED ME. I've got amazing hearing, my fleece has gone SUPER-soft and SUPER-strong, and ... OH! My spit! All llamas can spit, but I can spit a bucket of water over half a mile."

A.D. boggled. "As much as that?"

"Yep! See that weather vane?" Lola nodded to one in the shape of a cockerel on top of a distant church, then – "PTUI!" The super-charged spit sent the iron cockerel spinning so fast that it fell from the roof. Lola's long ears twitched and then she groaned. "Oh dear. Sounds as if the weather vane has hit someone on the head. Things ALWAYS go wrong when I use my powers.

- - - - -

That's why I carry these blankets, made from my own wool." She presented one to A.D. "I give them to people to help them mop up my spit."

"Well, thanks." A.D. dried himself with the blanket. It *was* super-soft. "Since someone singed my cape" – he gave Neon Zebra a look – "I will wear this to give myself some Mexican flair."

"Ooh, it suits you." Lola gave him a wink. "Now, I must find the person with the sore head and give them a blanket too. Bye!"

"Wait," said Ziggy, trotting after her, while

- - - - -

A.D. waddled behind. "The same thing happened to us. We both got powers from a meteorite."

"Really?" Lola turned in surprise and stumbled against a market stall selling the Power Pug piñatas. One fell to the ground and she frowned at it. "Hey, I recognise that little smooshed-up face."

"Well, *duh*," said Ziggy. "Power Pug's ugly mug is on all Poocho products."

"No, no, no," said Lola, shaking her head. "I mean, I saw him here this morning – talking to a **giant armadillo!**"

- - - - - -

4

Super-Spitting Sidekick

"YOU SAW **POWER PUG**?
HERE?" Adventure Duck stared up at Lola.
"Are you sure?"

"Sure as spit," said the llama, spraying
them with saliva. "He was talking to a big,
hairy armadillo in a beret."

"You know what this means, A.D.?" Ziggy
wiped her eye. "Armando the Commando
must be Power Pug's latest hench-animal!"

- - - - -

51

"So that's why his eyes were bright green," Adventure Duck realised. "He must be under Power Pug's **mind control**."

"If you say so," said Lola, turning. "Now, I really must get going ..."

"*WAIT!*" Ziggy followed after Lola. "Did you hear what they were talking about?"

Lola thought, waggling her ears. "The little doggy said something about meeting the armadillo at the chocolate plantation when the work was done."

"Yeah, right – the work of destroying

- - - - - -

chocolate shops. But why?" A.D. glanced back at the Power Pug piñatas. "Poocho, Inc makes chocolate bars – and those ugly things are stuffed full of their sweets. Why would Power Pug want to stop shops selling his own stuff? It doesn't make any sense."

"Who knows what that evil little mutt is up to," said Ziggy fiercely. "But as superheroes, it's our duty to stop him."

"You're superheroes?" Lola reared up so far she almost dropped her woolly blankets. "*¡Ay caramba!* That is so cool! I wish I could use my superpowers to help people."

- - - - -

"You've helped us already," Ziggy said with a smile. "Now we'll help you find someone in need of a blanket."

"You two go on," A.D. told them. "I'm going to talk to Yoki."

"Yoki?" Lola blinked. "Who's that?"

"It's complicated," said Ziggy. "I'll explain on the way."

Adventure Duck concentrated, sending his thoughts all the way back to the Underpond. "Yoki? You there?" He heard a flushing sound. "Oh, sorry. Did I catch you on the toilet?"

- - - - - -

"Um ... all places are as one to me," said Yoki calmly. "So, in a way, all places are the toilet."

"I *TOTALLY* caught you on the toilet, didn't I?" A.D. beamed. "Now, listen. I know our minds are linked by that Egg-stra Sensory Perception thing ... so did you see that giant armadillo that Zig and I fought?"

"I did." The image of Yoki appeared in front of A.D. "It looked rather hairy."

"Well, it turns out he's working for

Power Pug," said A.D., scowling. "He's been trashing the rainforest and destroying candy stores. He's going to meet Power Pug at a chocolate plantation."

Yoki's moustache waggled. "I shall use my mystical powers to locate the most likely address."

"Nice one!" said A.D. "How long will that take?"

"**Time is an illusion**, young duck."

A.D. groaned, shook his head, and set off after Ziggy and Lola.

He found them a short distance away, near the church. An old lady with a bump on her head was watching, baffled, as Lola spat all over her car, then wiped it with her furry butt.

"The lady didn't want a blanket so I'm washing her car to say sorry instead," Lola explained.

"Uh-huh." A.D. looked at the sticky smears and clumps of llama wool all over the bonnet and windscreen. "Nothing says sorry like ten litres of spit and a ton of fluff. Where's Ziggy?"

"Here! I've been watching the news." Ziggy

- - - - -

burst out of a nearby electronics store. "Armando the Commando just flattened El Cocoa Loco – the last remaining candy store in Mexico."

"We'd better head there," said A.D., "and see if we can stop him before he gets to the chocolate plantation."

"But what do we do then?" Ziggy looked worried. "Two of us couldn't stop him last time."

"Perhaps," said Lola, smiling shyly, "three of us could try."

Ziggy and A.D. turned to look at her.

"YOU?" asked Adventure Duck, surprised.

"I want to help people," said the llama. "I already have a superhero cape – and a cool name ..." She pulled a blue blanket from the bottom of the pile and opened it out. Emblazoned in yellow thread were the words **Señorita Spitfire**. "Ta da! You see? You like?"

"Adventure Duck, Neon Zebra and Señorita

Spitfire," said A.D. "Hmm. Maybe we could all work together."

"You mean it? YAYYY!" Lola spun around, swishing her cape. "So, how do we chase this armadillo? Do we run? Catch a bus? Borrow the old lady's car?"

"No need!" A.D. passed Lola his Jet-Shades. "We'll fly, like all sensible superheroes."

"Fly? Me?" Lola put on the dark glasses and pressed the button. "**EEEEEEEEK!**" She flew straight into a wall, then bounced off and knocked over a traffic light before belly-flopping on to the pavement with her long legs sprawled out.

"A hero is born," A.D. sighed. "Come on – let's get quacking!"

Hot on the Trail

Within minutes, the three animals
were flying in a **V-FORMATION**:
Adventure Duck out in front and Neon
Zebra helping Señorita Spitfire to stay
steady as they brought up the rear.
The view was amazing, with quaint
little towns nestled in a vast landscape
of fields, rocky mountains and prickly
cacti. Further in the distance, A.D. could
see the lush green canopy of the tropical
rainforest.

Even without his Jet-Shades, Adventure Duck could fly incredibly fast – and it didn't take long to reach the candy store that Armando had flattened.

"It's like a chocolate pancake," said Ziggy, looking down at the remains.

But the armadillo was nowhere in sight.

"Guys!" Lola looped the loop, spraying enough saliva to water an orchard. "I can hear loud crashes coming from the rainforest."

"I bet it's Armando," said Ziggy. "Change of flying formation, team! Lola – I mean,

Señorita Spitfire – you lead the way!"

Beaming with pride, Lola steered them into
the dense, steamy rainforest. Much of it was
wild, but soon they came to an area where
the trees grew in long rows and bristled
with red, fleshy pods.

"**CACAO!**" said Lola, as they landed.

"**Kuh-cow?**" Ziggy echoed blankly. "Is that some kind of catchphrase?"

"No, it's the plant that chocolate comes from," the llama explained. "This must be a chocolate plantation."

A.D. fanned himself with one wing, trying to cool himself off. "Then chances are, Armando's meeting Power Pug here."

"**Uh-oh**," said Lola, her ears alert. "I hear something heading this way." The sound of something crashing echoed through the rainforest.

"It sounds like we've got company coming," said Ziggy. "Big company."

"Then we have two choices," said Adventure Duck gravely. "One, we stay and **Fight** ... or two, we find ourselves a beach house, crank up the air-con, order a ton of soggy tortilla chips and **PARTY ALL NIGHT**."

"Tortilla chips give me wind," said Lola, spraying saliva everywhere. "So, I say we fight."

"Great," sighed A.D. "I was, er, hoping you'd choose that."

"Let's surprise Armando when he arrives,"

said Lola. A.D. and Ziggy followed her through the cacao trees to the edge of the forest, where the plantation ended.

An eerie quiet had fallen over the forest. No birds sang, no monkeys hooted. Soon, Adventure Duck felt the ground trembling under his feet. "*GET READY*," he told Lola and Ziggy, bracing himself for battle ...

A mass of stampeding animals **BURST** out from the thick undergrowth ... and raced past them! A.D. and Ziggy dived for cover as **howler monkeys** and OCELOTS, white-tailed DEER and hog-nosed *skunks*, **frogs** and *EAGLES* and KINKAJOUS and all kinds of critters fled from the rainforest.

"Run for your life!" cried a frog as
it hopped past. "Our home is being
destroyed!"

Ziggy peeked out from behind some ferns.
"Those poor animals," she said sadly.

The sound of trees being uprooted
rumbled like thunder through the jungle.
The trees ahead parted, falling as they
were torn from the ground. Something
was approaching with horrible speed.
Finally, like a giant scaly bulldozer in a
beret, Armando came lumbering into view.
A tiny figure was riding on top of him.

"**Power Pug!**" muttered Adventure Duck.

The demented little dog was dressed like a jungle explorer, his stubby limbs sticking out from a tailored khaki suit, with a pith helmet strapped to his head.

Power Pug's eyes widened at the sight of

-----

his old enemies. *"HALT, ARMANDO!"* he wheezed.

With his green eyes glowing, the armadillo stopped obediently. "Yes, General Pug, sir!"

"So!" Power Pug put his paws together. "The **dull-witted** duck and the ~~electric~~ zebra. We meet

again." He tried to drop his voice to a menacing whisper, though it came out as more of a rasping cough.

"This time I will destroy you."

"Not if Señorita Spitfire has anything to spray about it!" said Lola, coating Armando and Power Pug in a shower of spittle.

"That's right, pug-pants, we've got reinforcements," said A.D. "Whatever you're up to, **WE'RE GOING TO STOP IT**."

"Is that so? Well, according to the law, **YOU** are the bad guys here ..." Power Pug grinned nastily. "You see, the three of you are on private Poocho property! This is the biggest chocolate farm in the world. It belongs to **ME** ... and trespassers will be *PUNISHED!*"

Rumble in the Rainforest

While A.D., Ziggy and Lola stared at
in each other in alarm, Yoki's voice
suddenly boomed through A.D's head.
"SUCCESS!" he cried. "The Poocho
Inc, plantation is located at ... Oh. You're
already in it."

"Yep," A.D. muttered, "we're right in it!"

"I don't get it, Pug," said Ziggy. "If you own
this chocolate farm, why are you making

your pet armadillo destroy the rainforest around it?"

Power Pug smiled nastily. "Because once the area is razed to the ground I can expand my business."

"**WHAT?**" Lola looked shocked. "But isn't the land protected? What about all the endangered animals living there?"

"Who cares?" The pug did a jig. "My chocolate farm will be the

BIGGEST IN THE WORLD!"

Ziggy looked confused. "But if you want to make more chocolate, why have you been destroying all the chocolate shops?"

"You **pea-brained** zebra!" the pug scoffed. "Those shops were selling chocolate made by my competitors. Now I shall make sure they only buy **MY** chocolate ..."

"And I will travel the world," said Armando. "Destroying chocolate farms in other countries ..."

"... so that all other cocoa companies will go out of business!" Power Pug concluded, his eyes agleam. "Eventually, Poocho will supply ALL the chocolate in the world. Chocolate

I shall make so delicious, so sweetly addictive, that people will do anything to get it. A N Y T H I N G."

"I see where this is going," said Adventure Duck. "First you get everyone hooked on your chocolate, then you cut off the supply. They'll do anything you say to get more of the stuff."

Neon Zebra nodded nervously. "You'll have millions of people under your control."

"And I shall use them to help me TAKE OVER THE WORLD!" Power Pug laughed wheezily. "They shall overthrow the old world order ... and put ME in charge!

- - - - - -

"**A·HA·HA· HA·HA·HA!**"

Señorita Spitfire's face darkened with fury. "You are a bad, bad dog – *PTUI!*" She spat in disgust – and the gob-water knocked Power Pug's helmet right off his head.

"How **DARE** you!" squeaked the pug in outrage.

"Come on, my super-friends," Señorita Spitfire went on. "**LET'S WHUP HIS UGLY LITTLE BUTT!**"

"Good idea," said A.D. "Um ... any songs of defiance you're dying to share, Zig?"

"Always!" Neon Zebra charged up her stripes: *"Pug and armadillo! Pug and armadillo! We're gonna knock you down, and we won't give you a pillow!"*

Power Pug merely smirked, then turned to Armando with swirling eyes. "What do you say to that, my puppet ... ?"

"Uh-oh," A.D. gulped. "The pug's powering

- - - - -

up his mind control! His eyes are
hypnotising Armando."

The armadillo's eyes turned green
and swirly. "**Duck, zebra, llama -
Armando's gonna HARM YA!**"

Power Pug clapped his little paws
together with glee. "*ATTACK THEM
NOW!*"

"**Yes, General Pug, sir!**" The giant
armadillo lumbered forwards with
surprising speed and his tail came
whistling towards A.D.'s head.

"**DUCK!**" Ziggy shouted.

- - - - -

"Yes?" A.D. replied – and the tail cracked into his skull. With a dazed "*QUACK!*" he went flying backwards.

Señorita Spitfire spat at Armando like a fire hose, but the saliva bounced off his armoured shell. Power Pug hid in the scaly crevice between the giant armadillo's head and neck. "Surrender, you fools," he cried. "You cannot harm us."

"Maybe not, *but it's fun to try!*" Neon Zebra blasted Armando with blistering electric energy, but it had no effect. Desperate, she pressed a button on her Jet-Shades and shot towards the armadillo at super-speed. She struck him with all four hooves.

- - - - -

"OOF!" Armando quickly rolled over, flattening another tree and throwing Power Pug clear.

"YOU CLUMSY OAF!" the little villain shrieked as he tumbled through the air ... into Adventure Duck's waiting wing! **BASH!** The punch sent the pug spinning into the branches of an uprooted tree.

At the same time, Armando raised his head and let out a weird, ear-splitting howl like a broken siren.

"Huh?" Ziggy frowned. "I didn't think I hurt him that much."

"You did great." A.D. beamed at her. "You too, Lola!"

"Great?" sneered Power Pug. "You were lousy. **AND NOW, I SHALL CRUSH YOU!**"

"Oh, yeah?" jeered Ziggy. "You and whose army?"

The pug smiled nastily. "The one that's on its way right now!"

"Er, guys?" Lola was looking about, ears pricked. "Guys, I hear something ..."

"Uh-oh," said A.D. "Me too!" He didn't need super-hearing to hear the ominous sound of little legs pounding through the fallen forest ...

Adventure Duck, Neon Zebra and Señorita Spitfire gulped as **hundreds of regular-sized armadillos** emerged from the trees and marched forward in formation.

"I told you I was a commando," said Armando grimly. "Here is my army. They'll do anything I say."

Power Pug nodded. "They fear his enormous size ... his raw power ..."

"And especially his **BREATH**," A.D. broke

in, waving a wing in front of his nose.
"PWOAR!"

Ignoring the insult, Armando raised his voice. ***"ARMADILLOS ... ATTACK!"***

The armadillo soldiers followed
their commander's order without
hesitation. Grunting and squealing,
they charged at the three
superheroes!

"GET BEHIND ME!"

A.D. balanced on one webbed
foot and spun about in
a tight circle, turning himself
into a feathery tornado. The armadillos

were whisked into the wind before they could attack, and whooshed away in all directions.

"Good thinking, A.D.," cried Neon Zebra.

- - - - -

84

But there were more armadillos to deal with! Another unit was attacking the heroes from behind.

"**PTUI! PTUI!**" Señorita Spitfire let loose with some extra-sticky saliva-splats, knocking ranks of scaly soldiers back like a water cannon. "We cannot hurt the little ones. They're not evil – they're just scared of that big bully."

"**They're not the only ones!**" A.D. admitted.

"I have an idea." Neon Zebra fired some electro-zaps at the ground in front of them, blasting out a trench. "Fill this ditch

85

with spit-water, Lola, and we'll make a
moat to keep the little guys away from
us!"

"*LITTLE GUYS LIKE ME?*"

Armando joined the battle on his hind
legs, claws raised like huge spears. He
swatted A.D. aside, then dug up the very
ground Ziggy stood on so she lost her
balance and fell. Dozens of armadillos
swarmed over her.

"SEÑORITA SPITFIRE TO THE
RESCUE!" Lola spat enough sticky goo to
wash Ziggy's attackers away – but more
armadillos appeared at once to take their
place.

- - - - - -

"We're outnumbered!" cried Ziggy. "We can't hurt them, but they can hurt us."

"*AND SO CAN I!*" Armando butted Señorita Spitfire with his knobbly head. She fell over backwards in a daze.

"Ooh! Pretty stars!" said Lola, and then her long eyelashes fluttered shut.

A.D. forced a path through the armadillos, his wings sweeping the critters aside. When he finally reached his friends, he grabbed each of them by the tail. "**Retreat!**"

- - - - -

87

he quacked as he ran off, dragging them along behind him. "**I repeat – RETREAT.**"

"Call yourself a duck?" jeered Power Pug. "You're a **CHICKEN!** *HA, HA, HA!*"

As A.D. ran away, pulling Ziggy and Lola behind him, the hateful pug's chuckles echoed in his ears. *Laugh it up, pug-face,* he thought, scowling. *You may have won the battle – but the war isn't over yet!*

HUNTED!

Adventure Duck dragged Lola and Ziggy out of the chocolate farm and into the deepest part of the rainforest, where trees still stood. Finally, sweating in the tropical heat and panting for breath, he stopped. Ziggy and Lola were waking up.

"Ugh, what happened?" groaned Ziggy. "I feel like I've been dragged by the tail through a cocoa plantation."

"Funny, that," said A.D. "Are you OK, Lola?

"I am **EXHAUSTED!**" Lola winced. "My body is bruised, but my pride is bruised even more."

"Not as bruised as my bum!" said Ziggy, turning around and showing her bottom to the other two. "Look, it's black and blue! Well, white and blue ..."

"Thanks for sharing." A.D. shook his head and sighed. "I **HATE** running away. We have to think of a way to stop Power Pug's arma-dillo-geddon!"

"Night is falling." Lola looked up at the sky. "Soon we won't be able to see where we're going."

- - - - - -

"Not necessarily." Neon Zebra lit
herself up bright green.
"TA-DAAAA!"

"STOP THAT!" A.D. tried
to hide her with his wings. "Power
Pug and every armadillo around will spot
you from miles away! They're bound to
come after us sooner or later."

"That's true." Ziggy switched off her stripes.
"Because we're the only ones who can warn
the world about their plan."

"Right." A.D. nodded. "Come on, let's make
a camp and get our strength back. We're
going to need it!"

- - - - -

Lola showed A.D. how to string his cape between two trees to make a hammock. It was delightfully soft and snuggly. She did the same with her own cape, and shared the hammock with Ziggy. Besides the occasional **thump** when one of them fell out and hit the muddy ground, the rainforest was eerily quiet.

A.D. found the hammock so irresistibly comfortable it was hard to keep awake. He yawned, his eyes feeling heavy. "So," he whispered, "how are we going to stop Power Pug's army?"

"Challenge the armadillos to a game of chess," Lola suggested.

- - - - -

"Are you good at chess?" asked Ziggy.

"No," Lola admitted. "But while they concentrate on the game, we can hit them with big sticks."

"We'd need about a thousand chessboards," A.D. pointed out sleepily. "And we don't have a single one!"

"What if we dig a big hole and cover it with leaves?" said Lola. "Then we lure Armando and his army here and – **WHOOSH!** – into the hole they fall."

Ziggy shook her head. "They're armadillos, they'd just dig their way out again."

- - - - -

"We'll line the hole with metal so they can't escape," said Lola.

"Metal from where?"

"I shall mine some ore from the rainforest and smelt it into iron."

"That *hole* plan smelt!" A.D. yawned, his eyes feeling heavy. "I guess I'll have to use my mind-link with Yoki to ask his advice. **YO, YOKI** - ARE YOU THERE?"

"As much as I am anywhere," said the egg's mystical voice.

- - - - -

"What should we do about the armadillo army?" asked A.D.

"You are **very close** to the answer," replied the egg mysteriously.

A.D. yawned again. "I **AM?**"

"Yes." Yoki chuckled. "Why don't you sleep on it?"

The soft-boiled guru might have said something else, but Adventure Duck didn't hear it because he was fast asleep in his soft, snuggly hammock.

The splintering racket of toppling trees woke A.D. from a deep sleep. "**Wake up!**" he quacked in alarm.

Ziggy and Lola were so startled they fell out of their hammock with a **DOUBLE-WHUMP!**

"We fell asleep!" A.D. groaned. "So much for working out a plan."

"It's your fault, Lola," said Ziggy, rubbing her eyes with her hooves. "No one could stay awake for long in one of your woolly blankets – they're **SUPER-SNUGGLY!**"

- - - - -

"I am sorry, *amigos*! I have messed up yet again." Lola's big eyes brimmed with tears. "Señorita Spitfire is really Señorita Snoozy-Pants! I have failed you – and now Armando, his doggy general and their troops are approaching!"

A.D. took down his hammock and tied it around his neck like a cape. "How close are they?"

"Very close," Lola said. "QUICK! Hide up this tree!"

A.D. helped Ziggy and Lola shin up a tree, until all three were perched at the top, above the rainforest canopy. Through the leaves they saw Power Pug enter the clearing with Armando.

"Time for some bowling," Power Pug announced. He clapped his paws together. "ARMANDO, ASSUME THE POSITION!"

The giant beast obediently curled up into a ball. With his stubby little front paws, Power Pug gave Armando a push and the armadillo rolled towards a tree just metres from the superheroes' hiding place. With a *CREAK* and a *CRASH*, the tree toppled on to the forest floor.

"STRIKE!" wheezed Power Pug,

jumping up and down with excitement. As his hench-animal uncurled himself and straightened his beret, Power Pug turned to him and said, "Now, Armando, tell your little armadillo soldiers to cut down all the trees in this whole area and stack the logs into piles. And I want a search party looking for that **dismal duck** and his **gormless gang**."

"*YES, GENERAL PUG, SIR!*" said Armando, saluting.

"Now, I must return to my mansion to perfect the final stages of my **evil master plan**," said Power Pug. He threw back his head and laughed

- - - - -

uproariously. "Today, *Master of Armadillos!*
Tomorrow, **Master of All Chocolate!**
And before long, **MASTER OF THE
WORLD!**"

Beware Alpacas Bearing Gifts

Still clinging to the top of the tree with her friends, Ziggy watched Power Pug exit the clearing. "That flat-faced flop is **CRAZY**."

A.D. nodded. "Tell me something I **don't** know."

"OK!" said Lola. "Llama poop doesn't smell."

"Nice," said A.D. "But I won't ask you to prove it!"

Armando called out below. Moments later his army of armadillos came running into view – holding miniature axes with their tails! They started chopping into the trunks, hundreds of little clattering **THWACKS** that made the trees tremble.

"If things get any scarier, you're going to find out a fascinating fact about duck poop too!" A.D. confided.

"At least all that noise means they won't hear us escaping!" Ziggy leaped into the next tree. "Come on, let's get out of here – **MONKEY-STYLE!**"

A.D. and Lola followed her through the

treetops, swinging from branch to branch until they finally crashed to the ground a safe distance from Armando and his axe-swinging troops.

"Wait. Why didn't I just fly?" A.D. slapped a wing to his head. "I'm still half-asleep!"

"I'm sorry. I did warn you that my blankets are irresistibly soft," said Lola sadly, through a tangle of fluffy legs.

"What I don't understand is, why didn't Yoki

-----

warn me?" said A.D., frowning. "He said I was close to the answer and that I should sleep on it ... Oh, wait a minute. **THAT'S IT!**"

"What is?" asked Ziggy, adjusting her headband.

"I HAVE AN IDEA FOR HOW WE CAN SORT OUT POWER PUG!" It was all A.D. could do not to quack for joy. "And, Lola, don't be sorry – because we totally can't do this without you. How quickly can you knit a poncho, a hat with ear flaps and another hammock ... ?"

Lola turned out to be a nifty knitter, using two sharp twigs as knitting needles. She could even knit while moving stealthily through the jungle in search of Power Pug's mansion. Using her own woolly fleece – and keeping a cool head under pressure – she knitted steadily while dodging angry armadillos.

"**BRILLIANT**," said Ziggy, eyeing her woollen creations as they neared the fancy wooden building in the centre of the chocolate farm. "Now, are you sure you understand Adventure Duck's plan?"

"Of course." She put on the poncho, spitting merrily as she spoke. "And I will

- - - - -

wear the special sunglasses so Señor Pug cannot hypnotise me with his eyes."

Dodging Lola's saliva as best he could, A.D. plonked the hat on her to cover up her ears. "Then all we can say is ... good luck, Señorita Spitfire!"

"No, no. Now, I am undercover." She winked. "Call me ... **SEÑORITA FIRESPIT!**"

"I've had enough of you firing spit, thanks!" said A.D. "**NOW, GET IN THERE!**"

Lola made her way over to the office.

"Check that disguise," said Ziggy proudly.

- - - - -

"In that poncho,
funny hat and shades,
she looks—"

"Like a llama in a
poncho, funny hat and
shades," A.D. concluded.
"But Power Pug doesn't
know Lola as well as
we do. Let's hope she
gets away with it!"

Lola knocked on the mansion's front door.
Power Pug opened it, wearing a velvet
smoking jacket. "Who are you?" he asked.

"I am a poor, travelling hammock

seller," said Lola in a deep voice with a strange accent, trying hard not to spit. "I am giving away free samples of my hammocks."

"**HAMMOCKS?**" Power Pug echoed. "You're giving them away for **FREE?** That's a **TERRIBLE** business plan."

Lola sighed dramatically. "This is why I am poor."

"Wait a moment." The pug turned his big brown eyes on her and sniffed her suspiciously. "Aren't you the llama that was working with my enemy, Adventure Duck?"

"Um, no," said Lola, "I'm actually an alpaca. Don't worry, it's an easy mistake to make."

"**MISTAKE?**" screeched the demented dog. "**I AM POWER PUG. I NEVER MAKE MISTAKES**."

"Of course not," said Lola hastily. "Which is why you will not turn down such a fine free hammock as this! Let me prepare it for you ..." While A.D. and Ziggy watched from the bushes, holding their breath, Lola tied the hammock between two pillars on the front porch. "Here you go. Try it out."

"Well ..." Power Pug stroked the soft

woollen hammock with his paw. "I suppose I am quite exhausted. It's **HARD** to be a super-villain, run a vast business empire and keep a giant armadillo hypnotised." He scrambled into the hammock, wheezing with the effort. "Hmm. It's quite comfy, I suppose."

"It is indeed, you big-brained pooch," said Lola, gently rocking the hammock. "**VERY COMFY**."

"Amazing ideas are always sparking through my head, you know. Plans for world domination keep me awake ..." Power Pug yawned noisily. "I am always thinking ... thinking ... *ZZZZZZ Z*."

- - - - -

"It worked!" A.D. quacked. He and Ziggy ran and waddled over to hug Lola. "**WELL DONE!** That dumb pug couldn't stay awake in your super-soft hammock, same as us."

"And he'll regret it." Ziggy grinned as A.D. helped her fold the hammock around the pug's stocky little body. "Look at him! He's like a little burrito."

"And perfectly prepared for the next stage of our plan," said A.D. As Lola placed her Jet-Shades over Power Pug's eyes, A.D. contacted Yoki by ESP. "Hey, Egg. You can steer these sick shades you invented by

- - - - - -

remote control, right?"

Yoki cleared his throat. "Do you mean, can I guide the wearer of my Jet-Shades with my mesmerising mental powers?"

"Whatevs. You can do it, right?"

"Of course, young duck."

"**GUYS!**" Lola broke in. She had taken her hat off and her ears were rotating like satellite dishes. "Armando and his armadillo army are marching this way!"

"Then ... this is it, everyone." A.D gulped hard. "**THE FINAL BATTLE!**"

- - - - -

A Desperate
Plan

As the sound of marching feet rumbled through the chocolate farm, the three *amigos* prepared for the most dangerous stage of their plan. Neon Zebra switched on her stripes, which burned bright orange. Lola dumped her poncho and straightened her Señorita Spitfire cape.

Adventure Duck picked up Power Pug. The pooch was snoring softly, still swaddled in the blanket from head to paws.

- - - - -

"Are you going to hold him hostage to force Armando to keep away?" asked Ziggy.

"Nope." A.D. switched on the special shades that Power Pug now wore. "I've been using my head ... Now I think it's time we used **HIS!**"

Armando burst through the cacao trees, his beret still neatly in place. His armadillo army marched in formation behind him.

"**There you are**," boomed Armando. "**Troops – prepare to attack!**" The armadillo soldiers obeyed his order, immediately assembling into neat rows.

- - - - -

A.D. smiled at them all. "I have a word of advice for you lot," he said. *"DUCK!"*

Power Pug's Jet-Shades flared into life and the well-wrapped pooch shot into the ranks of armadillos like a furry guided missile! He knocked them down like hundreds of little armoured pins.

ZZZZZZOOOOMMMMMM!

"NICE FLYING, YOKI!" A.D. said.

"**GENIUS**," said Ziggy. "Wrapped in Lola's fleece, Power Pug doesn't hurt the armadillos as he takes them down!"

"But what about the big guy?" Lola pointed out.

Armando was trying to catch Power Pug – the demented little dog had woken up and was howling in fury. "**Help! Noooooo! This is an outrage!**"

the dog wheezed, whirling through the armadillo ranks, butting them aside.

"Armando! Crush those detestable super-animals. Destroy them!"

"Yoki!" A.D. called out. "Any suggestions for how we take down the big guy?"

"Size is an illusion," said Yoki's voice in his mind. "REMEMBER, ALL CREATURES HAVE A WEAK SPOT."

"I don't," said A.D. smugly. Then a vicious little armadillo bit him on his foot. "*OUCH!* OK, maybe I do." He flicked the critter away and turned to his friends. "Think, everyone.

- - - - - -

What's Armando's weakness? Besides his horrible fashion sense and poor oral hygiene."

"I know!" Ziggy gasped. "It must be the one bit of him that's not armoured – **HIS SOFT, HAIRY UNDERBELLY!**"

"Of course," said Lola. "But Armando will never bare his belly to us."

"Not on purpose," Adventure Duck agreed. "But I think I know how we can make him. Let's get back to the place we camped out."

"But the armadillos will have cut down all the trees there by now!" Ziggy protested.

- - - - -

"**PRECISELY!**" A.D. grinned as he took off into the air. "Come on!"

But Armando was already rolled up and ready to launch his attack. "**Stand by for crushing.**"

"Now, now, sweetie." Señorita Spitfire jumped into his path. "You don't want to harm a llama, do you?"

But apparently, he did. Armando bellowed with rage and charged forward like a wrecking ball. Neon Zebra blasted him with a crackling crescendo of electric energy, enough to knock him off course and send him flying into the air like

- - - - -

King Kong's ping pong ball. He smashed
into Power Pug's mansion, turning it to
matchsticks.

"I SAID, COME ON!" A.D. shouted, flying off across the plantation.

As Ziggy and Lola ran after him, A.D. called down, "You'll find it's quicker by pug!"

"Ha! Brilliant idea," said Ziggy. "Hop on, Señorita Spitfire!" Lola jumped on the zebra's back, then Ziggy jumped on to the bundled-up pug and steered him through the forest after their feathered friend.

"WOO-HOO!" she cheered. "I've always wanted to go surfing!"

"How **dare** you!" raged the pug beneath her. "I am an über-pug, not a pug Uber!"

- - - - -

Ziggy blew a *RASPBERRY* right in his face.

Following Adventure Duck, the llama, the zebra and their complaining ride whizzed across the farm batting aside any armed armadillos in their path. When they reached their destination, Ziggy and Lola hopped off Power Pug.

"What do you think?" asked Ziggy. "Should we give him a tip?"

"Oh, yes," said Lola. She picked up Power Pug, tipped him upside down, then launched him back in the direction of the armadillo soldiers.

- - - - -

"Those critters have been busy," Adventure Duck observed. The dense patch of forest had become a clearing – the trees had been hacked down and chopped up by the armadillos, the logs then piled in stacks and tied securely with rope.

"Those poor trees," said Lola sadly.

"Don't worry, they're going to get their own back," A.D. promised.

A thundering sound and shuddering ground signalled Armando's arrival.

"I'll distract him," said Adventure Duck, standing on top of the log pile. "Neon

- - - - -

Zebra, Señorita Spitfire – hide behind here and get ready to work together."

Moments later, the giant armoured ball that was Armando rumbled into sight. He pushed out his head. Taking a deep breath, A.D. swooped down from the log pile – and snatched Armando's beret in his beak!

"Give that back!"
roared Armando.

"Why? I think it suits me better." A.D. plonked it on his head and flapped about. "Hmm ... I bet it would look even better on my butt!"

- - - - -

"**NOOOOO!**" Armando's green eyes blazed with fury to see his beret perched on a duck's tail feathers. "**You'll pay for that!**" He uncurled fully and lunged for A.D.

TWIRL!

Adventure Duck barely dodged the beast's deadly claws in time. "Get ready, guys,"

-----

he called, landing in front of the log pile. "RIGHT – RELEASE THE RAINFOREST!"

Ziggy and Lola had already loosened the ropes around the logs, and now let go of them. The pile of logs came tumbling towards A.D. and Armando. At the last moment, A.D. soared up into the air – but Armando wasn't fast enough to get out of the way. The rolling logs knocked his legs from under him. He fell backwards and ...

"Soft underbelly alert!" Adventure Duck bellowed. "ZIGGY, LOLA – NOW!"

Justice is Sweet

As Armando fell on his back, he began rolling over to protect himself. But Neon Zebra and Señorita Spitfire were too fast! Ziggy fired a massive blast of hot-pink neon energy at Armando's tum, and Lola projected a stream of saliva that sizzled and steamed as it struck the blazing beams. Combined, the spit and sparks erupted into even fiercer energy that completely engulfed the giant armadillo ...

"Keep it up, partners!" Adventure Duck bopped Armando on the head with one of the fallen logs. "We've got to shock him back to normal ... we've just got to!" **BOP**! He biffed the armadillo again.

"**NO, STOP! PLEASE?** " cried Armando. He sounded different, somehow. "What is this sticky wet stuff all over me? **EWWWW!** And who's hitting me on the head? **WHERE AM I? WHAT'S HAPPENING?** "

"OK, that's enough," A.D. told his friends, tossing the log away. Ziggy and Lola stopped firing and collapsed, panting for breath.

Armando looked about confusedly, coated in a sticky, smoking sludge. The green light had gone from his eyes, and he looked highly alarmed. "Goodness me," he tutted. "Look at all this terrible damage!"

- - - - -

"I think it worked," Ziggy murmured to her allies. "He's not under Power Pug's control any more."

"IT'S A DISASTER!"

Armando squealed. "Who would hurt the rainforest like this?"

"I'm afraid that **YOU** did, Señor!" said Lola.

The armadillo's face fell, and not just because it was being sprayed with llama spit. "I did this?"

"In fairness, you were under the control of an evil pug at the time," A.D. added.

"I ... I remember a *strange little dog* coming up to me in the jungle ..." Armando sat up and tapped his head. "He stared into my eyes, but I can't remember anything after that."

"Well, I'm going to give Power Pug something to remember, all right," said A.D. "Yoki, can you send him our way?"

"Alas, young duck," Yoki said inside Adventure Duck's head. "I'm afraid I steered Power Pug head-first into a tree – and the impact made the Jet-Shades malfunction."

- - - - - -

"HELLLLL

High overhead, a small, swaddled figure
went corkscrewing through the sky at
incredible speed.

LLLLLP!"

"GET ME DOWN, I DEMAND IT! GET ME DOWWWWWWWN ..."

"Wow. Look at him go." A.D. smiled, waving Power Pug goodbye. "He could end up as the first pug in space!"

With Armando back to normal and Power Pug out of the picture, the animals got busy.

The giant armadillo rallied his smaller brothers and sisters and together they began to heal the rainforest, putting back the trees they'd uprooted and planting new ones.

"**YOU CAN COME BACK NOW!**" Adventure Duck boomed with his supersonic quack. "**THE RAINFOREST IS SAFE AGAIN!**"

- - - - -

134

One by one, the animals who'd been driven out from their homes returned. Birdsong, chirrups and chatter filled the tropical jungle once more.

"I wish I could put right all the bad things I was forced to do," said Armando, looking sadly at his red beret. "Knocking down trees and destroying candy stores! I FEEL AWFUL."

"Well, you can use your powers to look after the rainforests from now on," Lola suggested.

"I shall," Armando agreed, "with my armadillo friends to help me."

- - - - - -

"And what about you, Señorita Spitfire?"
said A.D. "You've proved that you're a
WORTHY SUPERHERO. Will you come back
to the Underpond with me and Zig, and
fight crime full-time?"

"Thank you ... but no. I love the sunshine
and warm weather too much to ever
leave." Lola smiled fondly at A.D. and Ziggy,
spraying them with spit as she continued,
"I will stay by Armando's side and look
after the rainforests with him."

"I wish you'd drench my back for once instead of my face," A.D. complained. "That would be ... well, water off a duck's back!"

"Oh, shush, A.D." Ziggy kissed Lola on her fleecy cheek. "I think it's BRILL you're staying here with Armando, Señorita Spitfire."

Armando stomped his army beret into the mud and growled, "THAT PUNY PUG HAD BETTER NOT COME BACK!"

"He'll have nothing to come back to, now we've foiled his plans," the smiling image of Yoki told Adventure Duck. "I hacked into the Poocho, Inc computer system and took money from the company's bank account.

- - - - -

I've given it to the owners of the chocolate shops he made Armando destroy so they can make repairs. They'll soon be open for business again."

"Power Pug caused the damage, so it's only right he pays for it!" A.D. declared. "Hmm, Yoki, that gives me an idea. D'you think you could hack into Poocho's computers again and get them to build a soggy bread factory without Power Pug knowing? And then, you know, put me in charge of it, as CHIEF TASTER?"

"NO," said Yoki, and he disappeared.

Adventure Duck sighed. "It was worth a try."

- - - - -

"Come on," said Ziggy, slipping on her Jet-Shades. "Let's get back to the pond. There's bound to be some soggy bread there for you."

"I've lost my Jet-Shades." A.D. waddled up to Neon Zebra. "Can you give me a lift home?"

"Sure." Ziggy nodded. "As long as you let me sing."

"Forget it!" said A.D. "I'll take the bus."

"That'll only take you a month or two. Tell you what, I'll take the bus with you – and sing all the way."

- - - - -

A.D. shuddered. "OK, OK, we'll fly."

A thought occurred to Ziggy. "Hey, do you think we should bring some cocoa back for Yoki?"

"What, and risk turning him into a chocolate egg? We might not see him after Easter." Adventure Duck grinned. "Ha – let's do it!"

"You're wicked," said Ziggy.

"Thank you," said A.D.

"Not that sort of wicked, you **STUPID** duck!"

"You can't take it back now, **STRIPY** ... !"

- - - - -

140

Armando and Lola laughed as, still bickering merrily, Adventure Duck and Neon Zebra took off into the warm Mexican skies, heading for home ... and for new adventures.

THE END

STEVE COLE

Bestselling author Steve Cole comes from a village with three different duck ponds. None of them has been hit by a meteor, but a duck did attack him once! When he's not writing funny stories, Steve performs with the pop band Faces Fall. Steve has a pet dog named Clara, who luckily does not possess evil mind-control powers. The superpower Steve would most like is the ability to conjure chocolate and chips from thin air (not always at the same time).

ALEKSEI BITSKOFF

Illustrator Aleksei Bitskoff was born in Estonia and loved to draw as a child, covering his school exercise books in doodles. He planned to become a teacher, but his travels brought him to London where he studied illustration instead. The superpower he would like most is self-multiplication, so he could be in lots of different places at the same time!

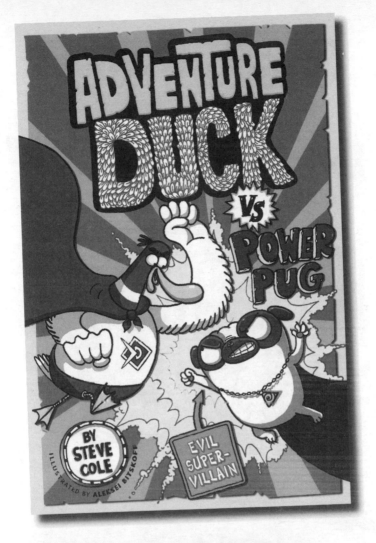

Coming Soon!

ADVENTURE DUCK takes on a cold-hearted villain in ...

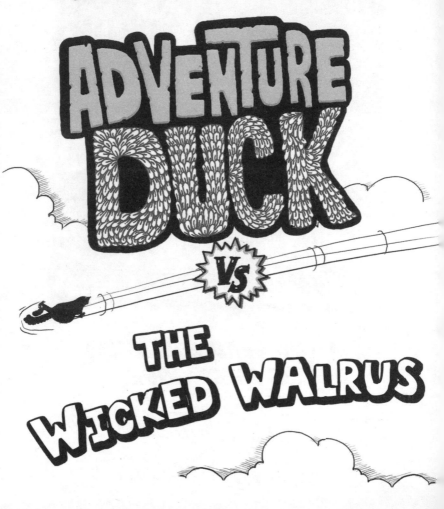